Mini Pizzas for Everyone!

Story by Jill McDougall
Illustrations by Ricard Zaplana Ruiz

Contents

Chapter 1

Party Food

"Soon, it will be the holidays,"
said Jon's teacher, Mr Lee.
"I hope you can all bring some food
for the class party, tomorrow."

"I could bring mini pizzas!"
said Jon.

Everyone cheered.
They all liked mini pizzas.

That afternoon,
Jon asked his big sister, Izzy,
to help him make some mini pizzas.

“I can’t make them by myself,” said Jon.

"We can make them together," said Izzy.

"We have to make a lot of pizzas," Jon said. "Everyone in my class will want one!"

Izzy and Jon began to make the mini pizzas.

Izzy cut up the tomatoes and green pepper. Then, Jon carefully put cheese, tomato and green pepper on top of the pizza bases.

The mini pizzas didn't take long to cook.
Soon, they were ready.

"They look great!" said Jon.
"And there is a mini pizza for everyone in my class."

Chapter 2

Too Late

When Dad came in from the garden,
he saw the mini pizzas.

"These look good," said Dad.
"I'll have to try one!"

He picked up a mini pizza and ate it.

"Dad!" cried Jon.
"The pizzas are for the people
in my class!"

But it was too late.

After that,
Jon's big brother, Daniel, came in.

"Mmm," said Daniel.
"I love mini pizzas!"

Before Jon could stop him,
Daniel began to eat one of the pizzas.

"Daniel!" said Jon.
"The pizzas are not for the family!"

"I'm sorry," said Daniel. "I was hungry."

Jon was not happy.
"Now there won't be a pizza for everyone in my class," he said to Izzy.

"It's okay, Jon," said Izzy.
"We can make some more mini pizzas."

Jon smiled. "Good!" he said.
"Now you and I can have a pizza, too!"

Chapter 3

The Class Party

The next day was the class party.

The children played games,
then they put the food out on the tables.

Mr Lee warmed up the mini pizzas,
and everyone ate one.

"I helped to make these pizzas,"
Jon told Mr Lee.

"You did a good job!" said Mr Lee.

"We could make mini pizzas
at school one day," said Mr Lee.
"Will you be my helper, Jon?"

Jon laughed.
"Yes!" he said.
"I'm getting very good at making them!"